RAINSTORM

To Rabbit

Copyright © 2007 by Barbara Lehman

For information about permission to reproduce selections
from this book, write to trade.permissions@hmhco.com or to
Permissions, Houghton Mifflin Harcourt Publishing Company,
3 Park Avenue, 19th Floor, New York, New York 10016.

www.hmhco.com

The illustrations are watercolor, gouache, and ink.

Library of Congress Cataloging-in-Publication Data
Lehman, Barbara.
Rainstorm / by Barbara Lehman.
p. cm.
Summary: In this wordless picture book, a boy finds a mysterious
key which leads him on an adventure one rainy day.
ISBN-13: 978-0-618-75639-1
[1. Adventure and adventurers—Fiction. 2. Play—Fiction. 3. Stories
without words] I. Title.
PZ7.L52176Rai 2007   [E]—dc22   2006049318

Printed in Malaysia
TWP 10 9 8 7
4500678855

RAINSTORM

Barbara Lehman

HOUGHTON MIFFLIN COMPANY BOSTON